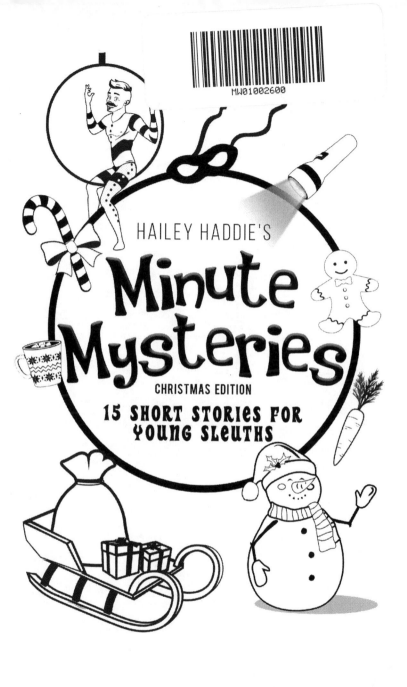

HAILEY HADDIE'S

Minute Mysteries

CHRISTMAS EDITION

15 SHORT STORIES FOR YOUNG SLEUTHS

First paperback edition November 2022

Written by Marina J. Bowman

ISBN 978-1-950341-93-1 (paperback)

ISBN 978-1-950341-94-8 (ebook)

Published by Code Pineapple

www.codepineapple.com

For aspiring amateur detectives with holiday spirit— you have been challenged!

Contents

Detective's Note

From present puzzles to frozen frost giants, I love to solve all mysteries! I may be known as the famous Hailey Haddie nowadays, but once upon a time I was just a young vampire detective with big dreams. Perhaps you even heard about me from junior crime solver Ellie "Scaredy Bat" Spark.

In the following pages, you will find a sampling of holiday-themed experiences taken from my case book.

In these accounts, every fact, every clue necessary to the solution is given. The answer is in the story itself. You need look nowhere else. Each problem has only one solution.

Written in three hundred words or so, these short stories can be read in about a minute and solved in a few more. The doodles that I have included may or may not be helpful for solving the mysteries.

I hope you will find them as enjoyable to read and solve as they were to write.

Good luck, detective!

—Hailey Haddie

The Case of the

Gone Gifpetta

I savored the warmth and sweetness of my peppermint tea as I waited in the café for Colin. My detective friend was almost always late for our coffee chats, so I ordered a cranberry scone while I waited. To my surprise, the clock framed by a poinsettia wreath struck one just as the door's bells jingled. Colin stepped in and instantly spotted me at my favorite table in the corner.

"Wow, it's a Christmas miracle!" I joked. "You're on time! Did Santa get you a watch for Christmas?"

Colin took a seat across from me and laughed. "I was almost late, but I was able to solve my latest household mystery pretty quickly. I'm telling you, if you want to keep things interesting, three kids will do the trick. Want to hear all about it?"

"Always!" I said, wrapping my hands around my toasty tea cup. "I love hearing about the shenanigans of Jones, Eve, and Kate."

My scone arrived, and Colin snapped off half before diving into his story. "Alright, so for Christmas I got them a Gifpetta Tree for the yard."

I nearly choked on my scone. "A Gifpetta Tree? You meant the ones that snack on small birds?"

Colin waved his hand dismissively. "That's just a rumor. So these magic trees grown by gnomes do like to snack, but not on birds. You can feed them vegetables and stuff—just not carrots, or they'll grow legs and walk away. But I'm getting ahead of myself. Anyway, so the kids have been bugging me for a long time for one. And I can't blame them. What kid wouldn't want a tree that grows presents underneath? This year it grew them each a pair of new mittens—which they loved but are bummed they haven't gotten to use yet because the weather has been too bad to go outside.

"So Kate is looking out the window this morning and screams, 'It's gone, it's gone! The tree ran away.'"

Colin shoved the scone in his mouth before continuing. "I go outside, and sure enough, it's gone. I dig around the area and find a half-eaten carrot. There are no giant tree footprints around—or any footprints for that matter—because it had been snowing so hard, but the tree had to have walked away. We had been home the past few days, so we would have heard someone drag it away to steal it. After all, it took me and three other people to bring it into the yard. Could have used one more person, but *someone* didn't answer my call."

"Hey, it's a busy mystery season," I said with a giggle and shrug. "I got your message too late."

"Sure, sure," Colin said, rolling his eyes. "You've always hated heavy lifting. Anyway, so I start by questioning Jones in his room. I notice a few things on his floor, including a carrot.

"Next, I go see Kate in her room. She says she thinks Jones did it because she saw him taking carrots out of the fridge last night. She has a wet sock on the floor, which could be from getting snow in her boot. But her friend's mom pulls up to bring her to karate before I can ask her any further questions.

"Finally, I visit Eve in the playroom. She is coloring pictures of the runaway tree. I ask her if she misses the tree, and she says no. She likes that it gave her gifts, but the tree is a little scary. Kate yells from downstairs, saying her new mittens are wet and asking if we have extra. I go downstairs, grab her a dry pair, and then go over all my interviews. I soon realize who did it."

"Ooo, this a good one," I said. "A little tough, but I figured it out."

"Sneaky little bugger," Colin said. "Want to help me put up 'Lost Tree' posters after this?"

Who fed the Gifpetta tree? How do you know?

HINT: If you carrot-all about this mystery, you won't concentrate on the vegetables.

SUPER HINT: At least one of the gifts got used.

The solution is found on page 92

The Case of the
Cookie Criminal

The tune of "Jingle Bells" flooded the cramped living room at my cousin Daisy's Christmas party. Some people chatted by the warm, crackling fireplace lined with stockings, while others danced to the merry music by the Christmas tree. But anyone who had been at one of Daisy's holiday get-togethers before knew the real party was at the snack table. Especially once her Top-Secret Chocolate Christmas Cookies were served later in the evening.

My mouth watered as I scanned the plates of desserts spread across the reindeer tablecloth. Crunchy, candy-coated pretzels, squishy marshmallow snowmen, a bowl of blood pudding topped with festive sprinkles—I didn't know where to start. Finally, I decided on a candy apple decorated with a black licorice belt to look like Santa's belly.

"Pardon my reach," I said to an old witch gumming a brownie. I removed my one fake fang and bit into the sticky treat, leaving behind a jagged, fangy bite mark.

The witch licked her dry, cracked lips. "Mm, I sure do miss those candy apples," she said with a slight lisp. "Luckily, these brownies are soft enough to mush up with my gums." She smiled, showing off her toothless mouth.

"I have dentures, but I can't stand wearing them."

"I think it would be worth it for Daisy's treats," I said. "Her candy apples are the best."

"But not as good as the blood pudding," said a woman with large blue eyes and a round face approaching the table. She showed off her glimmering white fangs as she held out her hand. "I'm Genie," she said. I gave her hand a sticky shake and introduced myself. A muscular man with a bald head glistening with sweat stepped behind Genie and browsed the goodies. "And this is my husband, William," Genie said.

William gave the old witch and me a small wave without looking up at us. His pale face turned green when his eyes locked on the blood pudding.

"I don't understand why you vampires love blood pudding so much," he said.

Genie giggled. "You humans eat it too, you know."

"But not extra bloody," said William. "Now, where are those Top-Secret Chocolate Christmas Cookies that you've been talking about for weeks? If they're as good as you say, I'd love to talk to Daisy about marketing them."

"They're not out yet," Genie answered. "But they're worth the wait! And please, try to avoid business talk for tonight."

"The cookies are cooling!" cooed Daisy. "I just took them out, so we have enough time for some carols. Come along!" Everyone except the three dessert-table dwellers followed the host to the snowy front yard. We were only five songs in when Daisy went back to the kitchen to fetch the cooled cookies.

"Oh no! They're ruined!" she shrieked.

All the party guests raced into the kitchen to find the Top-Secret Chocolate Christmas Cookies on the counter—each one with a perfect half-circle bite taken out of it.

"I chipped my fang earlier on a walnut, and now this?" whimpered Daisy. "This is turning out to be the worst Christmas party ever."

I narrowed down the suspects to Daisy, the old witch, Genie, and William, since they were the only ones in the house after Daisy left the cookies to cool.

"If it makes you feel better, I know exactly who the Christmas cookie nibbler is," I said.

Who is the cookie nibbler? And how do you know?

HINT: The proof is in the blood pudding.

SUPER HINT: People come in all shapes and sizes—and so do their bite marks.

The solution is found on page 93

The Case of the Expressive Elf

Christmas is my all-time favorite holiday, and no place does it better than Jellyfish Lake. Their Christmas Village is a winter wonderland with everything from a pine tree maze to catchy Christmas tunes to Santa himself sitting in a chair made of candy canes and marshmallows. You can even adopt your very own puggle—a round, fuzzy creature with buggy eyes. They live in vampire chimneys during the Christmas season to eat the debris to make room for Santa.

Nevertheless, my favorite part is always their ice sculpture competition. My grandfather used to take me to see it when I was a kid. I was always mesmerized by how a block of ice got chiseled into festive mermaids, leaping reindeer, and everything in-between.

I got myself a tall mug of fresh, hot cocoa to watch the competition. The delicious, chocolatey smell made my mouth water. However, my lips had barely touched its warm sweetness before my attention was diverted to an angry elf standing near Santa's chair. A hint of cinnamon wafted toward me as I approached.

"I did not!" screamed the elf, his heavy, dark eyebrows slamming together. He crossed his arms over his puffed-out chest. "She's a liar!" He pointed to a little girl with blonde pigtails and a purple scarf cowering behind a massive candy-cane pole.

"Now, now, Gubsie," Santa said to the elf. "Even if you did fart, it's not a big deal."

The elf shook his head. "I didn't. She's a liar, liar, pants on fire! She couldn't have even known if I farted because she's deaf. She couldn't have heard it."

The young girl's lip began to tremble.

"I believe the girl," I interjected.

The girl signed with her hands, explaining how she knew the elf farted—confirming my suspicion.

The elf's face flushed red. "Fine, I did it. But it's not my fault. It's that hot chocolate, I tell ya!" He apologized to the little girl. "I just didn't want to lose my spot in the Christmas Village."

How did the girl know the elf farted?

HINT: There is more than one way to detect a lie—and more than one way to detect a fart.

SUPER HINT: Sometimes it's easy to sniff out a liar.

The solution is found on page 94

The Case of the
Sleigh Slip-up

The strings of colorful lights dimmed, leaving only the sun's glow to illuminate the ice sculptures on the shore of Jellyfish Lake. Even though I knew the Christmas Village was closing, I couldn't pull myself away from the art pieces on the snow-covered beach. I admired the competition winner—a mermaid swimming up a tall Christmas tree—and then moved back to the runner-up—Bigfoot building a snowman with elves. However, it was the one of Santa disguised as a newspaper boy pulling a sleigh full of presents under a blanket that I kept coming back to. My grandfather used to tell me the story of Christmas when vampires were in hiding. Santa would dress up in disguises to deliver presents to vampire families to ensure he wasn't followed by vampire hunters.

"Ah yes, I do remember those times," Santa said behind me, as if reading my mind. "I'm glad my deliveries no longer require a costume change."

I laughed. "I bet! Traveling the world in one night is probably hard enough with one outfit." I glanced at my watch, realizing the Christmas Village had been closed for over twenty minutes. "Oh my, sorry to hold you up!" I apologized. "I'll get going."

"Actually," Santa replied. "If you aren't in a rush, I could use your detective skills, Hailey. There was an incident earlier today, and I want to get to the bottom of it."

My stomach bubbled with excitement. "Me, help you? I'd be honored!"

"Perfect!" Santa beamed. "Head up to my reindeer on McReary Hill over there, and I'll meet you in a few minutes."

I scratched under the soft chins of the reindeer and petted their thick fur as I waited. I giggled as Rudolph did a happy little butt wiggle when it was his turn for pets.

Santa soon came up the hill just as the sun began to set. He carried a large rolled-up rug over his shoulder. A short elf with curly blonde hair and a pointy chin followed. Santa stopped and dropped the rug into the snow. The elf bounced off Santa's butt.

"Whoops, didn't see that you stopped," she said. "Didn't mean to run into you."

Santa rolled out the rug with a punchy red striped pattern that popped against the fresh snow. Then, one by one, he hooked up the reindeer reins to the carpet.

"Don't you have a sleigh?" I asked.

Santa turned to the blonde elf. "Why don't you explain while I finish getting the reindeer tied?"

The elf obliged as she squinted at a reindeer rein and tried to knot it. "It was before sunrise when we left the North Pole this morning and we were getting ready to take off. I always push the sleigh to give it a boost, but today I pushed too early and it fell into the ravine below. I had seen Santa give the thumbs-up, so it's not my fault."

"I didn't give a thumbs-up. Why would I, when I wasn't ready?" Santa asked. The carpet began to hover off the ground as if enchanted by magic.

The elf shrugged. "Everyone makes mistakes."

I nodded. "And I think this time, *you* made the mistake. Something in your story doesn't add up."

What in the elf's story is unlikely and why?

HINT: Don't squint at the clues too hard.

SUPER HINT: Sometimes the most obvious clues are hard to see.

The solution is found on page 95

The Case of the

Present Puzzle

*K*nock! *Knock! Knock!*

It was Christmas Eve, and the pounding at my front door woke me from a deep slumber. I threw on a robe and my fuzzy slippers and went downstairs. The porch light revealed Mr. Tanner standing there in ratty, striped pajamas.

"What seems to be the problem?" I asked as I sleepily opened the front door.

"Oh, thank goodness you're home!" Mr. Tanner cried. "The presents from under my tree have been stolen. They were piled in my living room ready to open tomorrow morning, but now they're all gone."

I welcomed the shivering man inside and offered him a seat on the couch by the unlit fireplace. He shivered. "Why don't you light a fire?" he asked. "It's freezing in here."

"Melvin doesn't like the heat," I said. With a clank and clatter, two puggles fell out of my chimney. The basketball-sized creatures squealed with delight as they rolled over each other like furry little tumbleweeds in the pile of ashes. I clapped my hands, and they stopped, staring at me with buggy eyes. Their fur and soot made them look like fuzzy balloons that had been struck by lightning.

"Melvin! Marv! Can we have a moment of privacy?" I asked. The creatures looked at each other and then scurried back up the chimney, leaving behind a cloud of ash.

Mr. Tanner rolled his eyes. "I never understood adopting puggles for the Christmas season. Such a ridiculous tradition. Now, please, I came here about my missing presents."

"Are you sure they were stolen?" I asked.

"I'm afraid so," Mr. Tanner said with a whimper. "I was up in my bedroom about twenty minutes ago when I heard a noise. I rushed downstairs just in time to see a man dash out of the living room. I ran after him, but he kept casting spells back at me. He turned a chair into an alligator and a pebble into a boulder to try to stop me. Luckily, the spells were short-lived, and the objects turned back within a few minutes, so there was no danger to others.

"Anyway, the man jumped into a waiting automobile, and I trailed him in my car, which fortunately was in front of the house. But that slippery stealing snake got away from me."

"Did you get his license number?" I asked.

"No. Couldn't see it. When I lost him in the traffic, I drove right over here."

"Didn't you keep the house locked while you were upstairs?"

"Yes, but the burglar chiseled open a cellar window."

"Let me get dressed and we will go over and have a look," I suggested.

When I reached Mr. Tanner's mansion, I found a tree in the middle of his living room with no presents underneath. I went to the cellar window, which, sure enough, had chisel marks.

"Did you lock the front door when you ran out of the house?"

"Why—er," replied Mr. Tanner nervously, "the door locks automatically."

I sighed. "What are the chances you cheaped out and didn't buy presents this year and are now trying to cover it with a 'robbery?'"

Mr. Tanner gulped and turned pasty white.

"I just wish if you were going to be a grinch that you didn't wake me up to do so. I'm going back to bed."

How did I know Mr. Tanner was lying?

HINT: Solving mysteries doesn't require magic, just a keen eye for details.

SUPER HINT: What details would have been impossible for Mr. Tanner to know?

The solution is found on page 96

The Case of the
Christmas Circus

Ever been to a Christmas Circus? It's a lot like a regular circus but with glittery acrobats swinging from a thirty-foot Christmas tree like ornaments. All while clowns on stilts clumsily try to decorate the tree with oversized balls and ribbon. I mean, how can you not be clumsy walking on stilts? When one of the acrobats climbed to the top and did a handstand to put on the star, the crowd applauded wildly, including me. I almost forgot that I wasn't there to watch the show.

I followed detective Colin out of the noisy tent into the snowy field sprinkled with pine trees.

"You know how the circus people have been building a birdhouse for the bird sanctuary for Christmas?" he asked. My mind snapped to the four-foot-tall birdhouse of rainbow colors, and I nodded.

"Look over there," Colin said, pointing to a pile of rainbow rubble. "The fortune teller, returning from her psychic party at ten o'clock on Christmas Eve, found it bashed in, lying in the snow not far from the circus tents. She called me immediately, and I instructed her to see that nothing was disturbed. Arriving fifteen minutes later, I personally examined the ground so no clues would be destroyed."

I inspected the scene. There were no footprints, but there were a number of deep impressions about two inches square. It had been snowing all day until half an hour before the discovery of the broken birdhouse.

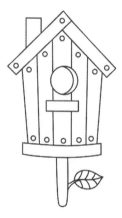

"These same imprints lead away from the broken birdhouse and end at the main road," Colin added. Headed to the road were four lines of these same impressions, about three and a half feet apart in length and about fourteen inches in width. In some places, however, they were badly run together.

"There were absolutely no other clues, and I could find no motive for the crime. It has me stumped," Colin said. "That's why I called you."

"Hmm, give me a little time to think," I said. "I'll call you at your hotel."

An hour later, I called Colin: "Look for someone who_____. Only such a person could possibly have committed the crime."

What did I say to Colin?

HINT: Solving this mystery is a tall order.

SUPER HINT: Don't let this mystery leave you stilted.

The solution is found on page 97

The Case of the
Troublesome
Transformations

My knuckles turned white as I gripped the armrest of the plane seat. My whole body shook from the turbulence that made the flight feel like a bad roller-coaster ride.

"I hate flying," I mumbled through gritted teeth.

"Oh dear, just do what I do and imagine it as a nice massage," said the woman next to me. The gray-haired woman had her eyes shut and a smile on her face.

"I don't think I can do that," I said, my stomach churning.

"Or pay attention to this lovely Christmas movie they are playing. It's about a little witch who wants to be an elf. So she disguises herself as an elf and gets a job in Santa's workshop. But her magic spells keep making things go wrong. It's very cute!"

I forced a smile. "Sounds fun, but I can't concentrate on a movie right now."

The woman looked over at me. "Hey! Aren't you that detective, Hailey Haddie!? My granddaughter, Ellie, loves you."

"Wait! Are you talking about Ellie Spark?"

"Yes!" I woman squealed. She took off her glasses and gave them a wipe. "She says you always get the best cases. What are you working on now?"

"I'm headed to see my best friend at her mountain cabin," I said. "So no mystery. Oh, but back home I did just solve quite the doozy before I left! There's a rich man named Mr. Tanner who is quite the old grump. His wife and daughter were making liver licorice garland to decorate the town tree in Brookside, but he wanted nothing to do with it and, instead, hid in his office."

"Ooo, are they the ones who make that delicious garland for the tree?" Grandma said, licking her fangs. "It's one of my favorite holiday treats! I can't believe someone would want to skip making such a fun Christmas decoration."

"I know!" I exclaimed. "But Mr. Tanner is a grump. That's part of why I wasn't surprised when Mr. Tanner was turned into a penguin in his study that night. You see, we've had this problem with wizards turning people into snowmen, reindeer, elves, and other festive creatures around the holidays.

"When I inspected his office, I noted it had multiple entry points—six windows, a back door, and the main entrance that opened to a corridor. At the other end of the corridor was a staircase that led to the servants' quarters above.

"I questioned Diodora Main, Mrs. Tanner's sister, who was staying at the house at the time of the transformation. While she appeared nervous, she insisted that she had been in her room at the time of the incident. Diodora's room is halfway between the office and the staircase to the servants' quarters.

"Layla, the maid, testified that as she was descending the stairs leading from the servants' quarters at midnight, she saw Diodora walking down the lighted corridor to the office. She was wearing a trench coat and her famous ruby pendant. A minute later, Layla heard Diodora and Mr. Tanner violently quarreling. She returned upstairs to the servants' quarters and, as she opened the door of her room, she heard the distinct bang of a spell being shot from a wand.

"In the face of such evidence, Diodora admitted having gone to the office at the time but insisted she was innocent—declaring she had remained only a minute.

"While Diodora was acquitted, she knew if the press got wind of the story, her reputation would be ruined. Luckily, I knew without further investigation that Layla's testimony was maliciously false. Diodora was so thankful, she insisted on gifting me one of those tree-decorating flashlights. You know, the magical lights that you just shine on your tree and it decorates it for you? I personally love decorating the tree myself, but it was nice of her."

"Ooo, how did you know Layla's testimony was false?" asked Grandma Spark. I explained, and she clapped her hands. "Bravo, young lady. And congratulations on making it through the flight."

To my surprise and delight, I saw the landing strip outside the plane window. Telling the story had distracted me so much that I hadn't even noticed we'd landed!

How do I know Layla's testimony is false?

HINT: Look at the story from all angles.

SUPER HINT: What could Layla not have possibly seen?

The solution is found on page 98

The Case of the

Festive Fibber

Twack! A snowball hit me right between the eyes. My vision blurred, my best friend's cabin on the mountain in the distance becoming a fuzzy pile of logs against the blue sky.

"Hey! We said no headshots!" I laughed as I wiped the snow off my chilled skin.

"Sorry, Hail," apologized my best friend, Aria. "You know I can't aim!"

"I hope you're better at decorating the tree than throwing snowballs," I said.

"Pfft, you know I'm the best decorator," said Aria. "As long as Sam dug out the ornaments from the shed, we can start decorating. I'll send a quick text to double-check."

5:50 PM

Aria: Did you bring in the ornaments from the shed outside?

Sam: Yup, did it yesterday when you asked. They're by the fireplace.

Aria: Perfect! Be home soon xo.

"Sam said they were brought in yesterday, so we're good to go!"

As a frigid breeze blew off the nearby mountain, I hugged my puffy coat. "Then let's head back, because I'm cold!"

After getting distracted by birds weaving in and out of the trees, we finally made our way back up the mountain to the cabin. It was only five minutes from where we had our snowball battle, but the uphill walk and frigid cold made it feel twice as long.

We walked into the cabin just as the reindeer clock struck six and his nose lit up red. The smell of chestnut and chicken macaroni and cheese made my taste buds tingle. Just as Sam had said, the ornaments were by the fireplace. I rubbed my palms together in front of the toasty flame trying to unthaw my fingers. Unfortunately, unwrapping the cold glass ornaments rechilled them almost instantly.

"Sam said supper will be ready in about an hour," Aria said. "Just enough time to get this done!"

Aria and I decorated the tree while Christmas tunes played over the radio. With only the star left to put on the top, Aria turned to look at me.

"So what do you think of Sam?" she asked.

"Seems nice," I said in a voice a little too high-pitched.

"That's your lying voice!" she said. "Why don't you like Sam?"

I sighed. "It's not that I don't like Sam—I just don't like that Sam lied."

What did Sam lie about and how do I know?

HINT: The answer will chill you.

SUPER HINT: Temperature-wise, something doesn't add up.

The solution is found on page 99

The Case of the
Wandering Wand

Sometimes I feel like mysteries follow me like a magnet. And that was certainly the case this Christmas season. I decided to take the train home from my friend Aria's cabin instead of flying. It seemed much more relaxing—until a mystery showed up.

Don't get me wrong, I *love* being a detective. But everyone needs a holiday now and then. Anyway, I had just settled down with a cup of black coffee at the train station. Equipped with the latest crossword and a novel, I was ready to kick back while I waited for my train.

Unfortunately, the superintendent of the train station had other plans for me.

"You! I recognize you!" he cried. I jumped so hard that I splattered coffee on the snowflakes dotting my Christmas sweater. "I hear you're a great detective, and it's a miracle you're here. Come with me!" A mixture of not wanting to be rude and curiosity led me to where a skinny man with a graying beard sat on the train step.

"Tell your story to Hailey Haddie," said the superintendent, introducing the conductor.

"Well," said James, "last night we left Albany hauling candy-cane cargo and passengers, including the entire Frost Giant Christmas Choir and Orchestra. It wasn't long before I heard a terrifying shriek a few cars back. At this

49

time, I was standing at one end of the car, the maid, porter, and brakeman at the other end. We met at the berth, where the beds are, and a Frost Giant stood frozen like a statue. Sometimes those guys only look frozen with icicles hanging off their huge bodies and beards, but this one really was! Must have been some kind of spell. Another Frost Giant named Biddy was in tears, wailing so hard the whole train shook. Apparently, the frozen giant was their lead violin player, and they have a big Christmas show this evening."

"And without the original wand that cast the spell, you can't reverse it," I added.

"Exactly," James said. "So I immediately had both doors of the car guarded as well as the doors to the washrooms. Every berth was occupied, and by this time the passengers were wandering around in the aisle.

"I began to look for a wizard wand capable of such magic. Every passenger, even the maid, brakeman, and porter, every inch of the car and all baggage were searched, but still we failed to find it."

"The windowsills were covered with freshly fallen snow, and an examination proved that none of them had been opened. No one had left the car, and no one had entered either washroom. I knew the wand must be in the car—but where? We never found it. You're welcome to look around the train for clues."

"No need," I said. "If you searched everywhere that you said you did, then there is only one place it can be." Sure enough, I was right. As a bonus, I solved the mystery quickly enough that my coffee was still hot!

Where did I find the wand and who is guilty?

HINT: Searching everywhere and everyone is always important.

SUPER HINT: Always conduct your investigations carefully.

The solution is found on page 100

The Case of the

Snatched Sorcerer

When the Brookside police get overwhelmed, they often call me to help them out. However, for whatever reason, I always end up with the strangest cases.

A mystery author with blue hair named Zora impatiently tapped her long red fingernails on the other side of the table. Newspapers and dust blanketed every surface, from the pullout sofa to the creaky old floor in the tiny guest house. I couldn't tell if the kidnap victim was just a messy witch or if she didn't have time to tidy, since she had just returned home an hour ago.

"Can we hurry this along?" Zora asked. "Not to be rude, but I never miss the Sunday Christmas Parade. I could really use the joy of floats and fireworks after what I've been through. And the parade starts in—" She looked down at her tarnished gold watch. "Ugh, I love this old thing, but I hate that it has to be wound every twenty-four hours. Do you have the time?"

"It's 4:36," I answered. "Don't worry, this won't take long. Why don't we dive right in so you can get to the five o'clock parade. Do you know why you were kidnapped?"

"People know that I can make spells from potions," Zora said. "So I've had someone kidnap me before, hoping I would brew them up a magic pink pony. This time was different, though—they wanted to know about the Fitzgeralds' secret Christmas cookie recipe."

I scribbled the details in my notebook. "Maybe start from the beginning."

Zora sighed. "I am going to miss this parade, aren't I?"

"No, no," I said. "Just a quick retelling will do. Then I will take you to the parade myself."

"I was doing Christmas shopping on Birnham Street around seven PM Friday when two masked men with wizard wands ordered me into a blue van. I was blindfolded, gagged, and my hands were tied behind my back. After they drove for about an hour, I was led into a house and down some stairs to a small room. After they removed my blindfold and gag, they questioned me at length about the Fitzgeralds' secret Christmas cookie recipe. I tried to tell them I didn't know anything, but they refused to believe me.

"Exasperated, they threatened to turn me into a reindeer with their wands. When I wouldn't give them any more information, one cast a sleeping spell on me, and I conked out.

"The next thing I knew, I woke up on the cold cement floor with a massive headache. I lay still for a few minutes and, hearing nothing but the ticking of my watch, I cautiously got to my feet and groped for the door in the dark room. Before I could locate it, the two men, still masked, entered. They clicked on the light, apologized profusely for the treatment I had received, and said they had mistaken me for someone else. They untied my hands and gave me something to eat. Then they blindfolded me again and drove me within a block of here. Before I could remove my blindfold after getting out of the car, it had sped away. That was about an hour ago. Now I'm here, and I don't know what to make of any of it."

I finished scribbling down my notes. "I just have one last question: How long have you been writing books?"

Zora shifted in her chair. "Not sure what that has to do with any of this, but only a couple of years. My debut mystery novel comes out next week."

I nodded. "Well, I sincerely hope you did a better job making up that story, because I'm not buying this one."

What flaw in Zora's story proved the kidnapping was fake?

HINT: Make time to check all the details.

SUPER HINT: Don't get ticked off if you can't solve it right away.

The solution is found on page 101

The Case of the
Float Fiasco

A float filled with Styrofoam mountains and Christmas trees for the Jotun Frost Giants. A float with crinkle paper waves and Christmas ball bubbles for the mermaids. A float stacked with presents and a throne for Santa and his elves. This Christmas Parade had it all—including a great mystery.

I followed my nose through the crowd to find the source of the delicious peppermint hot chocolate smell. It led me to a booth called Gnome Grown Hot Chocolate. Everyone knew that gnomes grew the best peppermint for tea, potions, and treats, so I didn't mind waiting in the long line. A short gnome with red braids, a summer dress, and winter gloves handed me the hot chocolate. I headed to find a blood pudding vendor next, but I never made it.

I stopped to admire the bouncy castle shaped like Santa's workshop. Giddy screams and laughter echoed from within the cushiony interior with ballooned walls colored to look like wood. I watched as two siblings, Garrett and Trixie, took turns trying to climb the candy-cane pole in the middle. Suddenly, a small, calloused hand tugged at the bottom of my coat.

"Hailey! I'm so glad to spot you," said the bearded gnome dressed in shorts and a t-shirt. I pulled my puffer coat around me tighter, never understanding how such small creatures could stay warm in the freezing cold without needing winter clothing. "You don't know me, but I'm Grenadier. Everyone says you're the best detective. So I knew as soon as it happened that I had to find you!"

"As soon as what happened?" I asked.

"It's our float! It's terrible. We made it plant-themed and decorated all the gnome plants with Christmas baubles and licorice liver garland. But now it's ruined!" He pulled me to the lineup of floats parked on the blocked-off street in front of the library.

"I don't see a green float," I said.

"Exactly," the gnome cried. "But do you see a purple one?" I instantly spotted the all-purple float globbed with thick paint. Everything from the fake Blumungous flowers to the Gifpettas were the color of eggplant.

"We just left for lunch for a few minutes and came back to this," the gnome whimpered.

"Do you know who might want to ruin your float?" I asked.

"Well, anyone with a float, really. We won first prize last year with our Gifpetta Christmas Tree."

"Ah yes, I remember," I answered. "Did anyone stay behind at lunch?"

"Sure, Weeger did. But he's always so tired. He fell asleep and didn't see any of this happen. Here, he can tell you himself."

I followed Grenadier to the back of the float, where the balding gnome with grey hair was curled up in a ball on a pile of scarves.

"Hey, Weeger!" Grenadier shouted, but the snoring gnome didn't budge. "Hey, Weeger!" he shouted even louder while clapping his hands. Weeger pulled a scarf over his face with one of his wrinkled hands and let out an extra loud snore.

"It's okay," I said. "I already have a good hunch who did it."

Who is my prime suspect and why?

HINT: The details in the mystery practically hand you the answer.

SUPER HINT: Sometimes the sweetest jobs can turn you sour.

The solution is found on page 102

The Case of the

Unexpected Unwrapping

With the power out in the whole town, I decided to spend my Christmas at Colin's with his kids. We enjoyed sweet treats and carols before we turned in for the night. Something about the gingersnap cookies made my stomach grumbly, though, so I tossed and turned a lot.

Three hours after we all went to bed, Colin's daughter Eve stood over my bed with a flashlight that highlighted her watery eyes and runny nose. I thought I was dreaming at first.

But as she hugged me and wiped her snotty nose on my chest, I knew I wasn't.

"Someone opened all the presents," she sobbed. "Every single one that Santa brought."

"Oh dear. Let's go see what your Daddy has to say," I said, not knowing what to do. As Colin tried to calm Eve, I nervously played with the wax of the candle sitting on his desk. It was still soft and warm, perfect for squishing into a little ball. We used Eve's flashlight to assess the damage; sure enough, she was right. Every one of the presents had been ripped open.

Colin put Eve back to bed and came straight to the living room to rewrap the gifts.

"Which kid do you think did it?" I asked.

"I'm not sure," he said. "Eve is always too excited to sleep on Christmas Eve, and Kate begs all the time to open presents early. Then there's Jones, who has unwrapped his gifts many times before the rest of the house is up. But never gifts that aren't his."

I took a sip from my hot chocolate mug on the end table from before bedtime. To my surprise, it wasn't sweet chocolate that hit my tongue but rather tingly peppermint tea. I put the hot mug back down, realizing it was Colin's and not mine, and got to work.

After walking the room a few times, I paused at seven Christmas cards ready for mailing: three gray, one green, two red, and one white. All the letters were closed with stickers of Santa.

"Did you forget to mail out Christmas cards?" I asked.

Colin groaned. "Yup. Things have been so busy lately. This time of year is always so stressful."

"Do you have trouble sleeping when you're stressed?"

"Sometimes, but I got new blackout curtains to keep the room dark, and it seems to help. I was so tired tonight that I fell asleep almost immediately. I didn't wake up until you and Eve knocked on my door."

I helped Colin wrap the last gift. "The good news is, I think I know what happened."

Who unwrapped the presents, and what clue tipped you off?

HINT: Shine a little light on the situation.

SUPER HINT: You'll need something warm before you're hot on the trail.

The solution is found on page 103

The Case of the

Hot Cocoa Hiccup

*D*ing. Ding. Ding.

I quickly straightened my dress and answered the video call. Santa with his white beard and red suit waved merrily at me.

"Hello, Miss Haddie! It's been a while. I was hoping maybe you had a minute to investigate something for me."

"Of course! What can I do for you?"

Santa lowered his voice to a whisper. "You see, someone has been drinking my hot chocolate. Now, I don't mind sharing, but it seems every time I make myself a fresh cup, it disappears as soon as I leave for a second! Just look at this." He held up an empty cup shaped like a polar bear to the camera. "Empty! And I only left it for a few moments when I went to go brush my hair for this call."

"That sounds awful," I said. "Do you have any suspects?"

Mrs. Claus walked into the background. "Oh my, I didn't realize you were on a call. So sorry!" She scratched her elbow as she gave me a wave.

"I was just telling Hailey how someone keeps stealing my hot chocolate." An elf snuck into the door behind Mr. and Mrs. Claus and nabbed a teddy bear before disappearing.

"Ah, yes, that really is a shame," Mrs. Claus said. "He makes it with fresh cream, and it is the absolute best! It's too bad I'm lactose intolerant. On top of making me have to go to the bathroom urgently, it always gives me this weird reaction where my arms get freckled and itchy. Anywho, I'll leave you to your call."

"Maybe you can stick around and help," I said. "I was just asking Santa who the suspects are."

"Oh. Well, there is Blitzen, who is always eating or drinking something. Just last week I found him slurping down my coffee," Mrs. Claus answered.

"I've never seen him move so fast," Santa laughed. "And then there is Rodney the elf. Still trying to teach him not to take things that aren't his. He's still little and learning but hasn't quite figured it out yet."

A loud grumbling came from Santa's side of the call.

"What on earth was that?" Santa asked.

"Sounds like the reindeer are hungry. I should go feed them," said Mrs. Claus. Blitzen appeared at the window, gnawing on an apple.

"No, no, let one of the elves do it," Santa said. "I want to solve this. Plus, look! He already has food." Blitzen disappeared.

"I think I have already solved it," I said.

Who is the hot-chocolate thief, and how do I know?

HINT: Some people never learn.

SUPER HINT: Sometimes not being able to have something makes you crave it more.

The solution is found on page 104

The Case of the

Conjuring Caper

Getting ready to unwind for my Christmas vacation, I kicked my feet up on my desk, took a bite of fruit cake, and opened my email. According to the cat clock on my office wall, in just one hour I would have two weeks free of mysteries. But until then, I really wanted to read my favorite newsletter, *Minute Mystery Brain Busters*.

This was their latest:

"Wanda hurried into the kitchen," said the assistant to Detective Bronco. "She told me she was called away unexpectedly and that I was to go to her apothecary and take the present potions

she made to the orphanage. Each one was sup-posed to conjure up ten presents so the kids had something to open on Christmas morning.

"Anyway, I was busy," he continued, "but in about five minutes I went through the hall, and, thinking I heard a noise, I stopped and listened at the apothecary door. There was someone moving about. The door was open. As I peered around it, I saw a masked man, wand in hand, hesitating near the fireplace.

"Then he went over to the table in the center of the room with a cash box. He picked up the stacks of ten- and twenty-dollar bills and left by the window. I called the police immediately and gave them a description."

"Exactly what time was that?" asked Bronco.

"Just about ten o'clock, sir."

"Had you been in the apothecary before that, this morning?"

"No, I hadn't."

"Humph," said Bronco as he pointed to a bill on the floor, "the thief dropped one." He picked up the crisp twenty and circled the room lined with shelves of potions and jars and tables topped with vials and flasks of colorful liquids. "I see your Wanda has quite the ingredient collection," he continued, glancing around the large room.

"I suppose she does," said the assistant.

"*I wonder if she can mix something up that would make you a better storyteller!*"

I laughed at Bronco's last line. And I knew exactly why he'd said it.

Why does Bronco think the assistant made up a story?

HINT: It's not always what you see.

SUPER HINT: You could say the assistant's number is up.

The solution is found on page 105

The Case of the Toasted Tree

I scanned the bookshelf in my office for any books that I wanted to take with me on Christmas vacation. The plan was two weeks of no work and no mysteries. And it was all happening in a mere hour. My stomach bubbled with excitement. At least I hoped it was excitement and not the obnoxious amount of fruit cake I'd eaten at lunch.

The phone on my desk vibrated as it rang, sending a pile of paper flying onto the floor. Cleaning up would have to wait until after my break.

"Hello?"

"Hi there, Hailey," said the chief of police. "We're swamped, and the Martindales have submitted a Christmas tree related insurance claim. Would you mind swinging by there before you head off on vacation?"

"Absolutely," I said. "Think I can finish it in an hour?"

The chief laughed. "Knowing you, I give it half an hour. Good luck!"

I hopped in my car and zipped down to the Martindales' house on the lake. The lake was frozen with a thick layer of snow. The light breeze lifted a small cluster of snowflakes, making them dance across the surface.

I knocked on the door of the brick two-story house with floor-to-ceiling windows. A woman in an ugly Christmas sweater featuring cats with bell collars opened it.

"We're so happy you could come," Mrs. Martindale said, throwing on her coat and boots from a closet stuffed with boxes of decorations. "The tree is outside." I followed her around back, where she showed me a black, burnt tree. The wood decking around the tree was also heavily damaged from the fire. I touched a branch, and it crumbled like black pepper onto the snow below.

"My husband dragged this tree out of the woods this morning. I guess one of the Christmas lights was faulty. Now we don't have a tree, and Christmas is ruined."

"I'm sure we can find you another tree," I said. "You live right beside a forest."

"Oh, but I don't want to bother any of those trees," she said. "They're just too pretty."

I instructed her to call Minford's tree lot in town as I walked around. I followed a set of footprints out to the woods. They led to a stump. I walked back and continued to question Mrs. Martindale.

"Do you normally cut down your own tree?"

"Yes, my husband cuts one down every year. It was extra hard this year since the wagon broke, so he had to drag it behind him all the way here."

"And where is your husband now?" I asked.

"He went into town to pick up groceries for Christmas dinner."

"Big party?" I asked.

"Always," she said. "The whole neighborhood comes over to enjoy our food and decorations."

"Do they also enjoy your lies?"

What clue tipped me off to Mrs. Martindale lying about the tree?

HINT: The story details have to line up with the clues.

SUPER HINT: The snow holds the answer.

The solution is found on page 106

IT STANDS TO REASON

A Mystery Game

Here is a fun game of wits for a party of any size. It can be played in either of two ways:

1. Select one or more stories from the Minute Mysteries that sound interesting. Make as many copies of each as there are guests at the party. Then pass the copies around and allow a few minutes for your guests to study them. At the end of this time, each must hand you a written solution with the reasoning behind it. Compare these with the solutions at the back of the book; the one who is most often correct is the winner!

2. Instead of making copies of each story, you may read it aloud, slowly and carefully. It may be read a second time, if necessary. But after this, no questions may be asked. After the time limit has passed, each guest writes out their solution as in (1), and hands it to you for comparison with the solutions at the back of the book.

Method number one puts the emphasis on one's powers of reasoning and analysis; method number two adds to these a focus on an accurate memory. Let the games begin!

Mystery-Solving Tips

Some of these mysteries involve a 'crime' and a 'culprit.' Use the below prompts to take notes as you read and solve each mystery!

Name: Write the name of the suspect, witness, or victim

Motive: Write the reason why a suspect might have committed the 'crime'

Access: Write the time and place it happened

How: Write the way the suspect could have committed the 'crime'

Clues: Write any observations or details that may support the motive, access, or how

Get the Suspect Template at:

scaredybat.com/mm-template

MYSTERIES SOLVED

1. GONE GIFPETTA

Kate fed the tree. I know because her new mittens were wet, yet Colin states she hadn't gotten to use them yet because of the bad weather. As for the carrot on Jones' floor? Turns out the kids just like to keep snacks handy.

2. COOKIE CRIMINAL

William was the one who took a bite out of all the cookies—his human bite mark is the only one that matches. The old witch had no teeth to bite. Additionally, it was established that both Daisy and Genie had vampire fangs, which make a jagged bite mark. We know from his blood pudding conversation at the table that William is a human—most of whom make a half-circle bite mark.

William later confessed. He wanted to convince Daisy to box her cookies with the story of the mysterious Christmas cookie nibbler. The slogan? *One bite, and you're hooked.*

3. EXPRESSIVE ELF

The little girl didn't need to hear Gubsie fart
to know he did it—she could smell it. Luckily,
elf farts smell like cinnamon!

4. SLEIGH SLIP-UP

The elf had difficulty seeing the reindeer reins and Santa stopping right in front of her with some light still left in the sky. It's highly unlikely that she would see Santa give the thumbs-up in the dark, early hours of the morning with her bad vision.

I later learned she didn't want to admit she couldn't see because she loved being the one to push the sleigh. Thankfully, Santa's elves have the best healthcare plan, and a good pair of glasses fixed her vision problems.

5. PRESENT PUZZLE

If Mr. Tanner were pursuing the burglar, he could not have known the alligator and boulder turned back after a few minutes. Additionally, he wouldn't have known about the chiseled window. After all, he said he drove right over after his car chase. Of course, I could have solved this without going to Mr. Tanner's house, but I figured since he woke me up, at the very least I could finally see the inside of his famous mansion.

6. CHRISTMAS CIRCUS

I said, "Look for someone who can use stilts. Only someone on stilts could have made the marks in the snow you described."

P.S. I was right! A clown accidentally knocked the birdhouse over while practicing on stilts, but didn't want to tell anyone.

7. TROUBLESOME TRANSFORMA-TIONS

With the setup of the office and corridor, Layla would have only seen Diodora's back as she walked to the office. It would have been impossible to tell she was wearing her famous ruby pendant. Even if she could have identified it from the chain—which is unlikely—the trench coat collar would have covered it on the back of her neck.

8. FESTIVE FIBBER

Sam lied about bringing in the Christmas decorations yesterday. If the decorations were brought in sooner, they wouldn't still be freezing cold, especially sitting near the fireplace.

9. WANDERING WAND

Every piece of baggage had been examined and every inch of the car inspected. All passengers, even the maid, porter, and brakeman, had been searched. The wand had to still be in the car.

Remember—there was nothing said about James the conductor being searched. The wand was found in his pocket. Biddy had paid him to cast the spell on the other Frost Giant so she could be the lead violin player in the Christmas show. Unfortunately for her, he was unfrozen as soon as the conductor's wand was found, and she was kicked out of the show.

10. SNATCHED SORCERER

If Zora wound her watch immediately before seven PM Friday—the time of her alleged kidnapping—it would not have been running Sunday afternoon when she recovered consciousness and said she heard it ticking. The watch has to be wound every twenty-four hours.

She later confessed that a man named William from her PR team thought the kidnapping story would help sell more books.

11. FLOAT FIASCO

My hunch told me that the gnome selling hot chocolate did it, and I was right! Even though she was wearing summer clothes in the cold, she had on winter gloves. I thought maybe gnomes' hands got cold but noticed none of the other gnomes were wearing them. Sure enough, she had to put on gloves because she had stained her hands with purple paint. You could say I caught her purple-handed!

She later confessed she ruined the float because she hated that she never got to ride in the parade and was always stuck handing out hot chocolate.

12. UNEXPECTED UNWRAPPING

Colin unwrapped the presents, and his candle and tea mug were the clues. He said he fell asleep right away—three hours before Eve woke me up. Yet, if he sleeps in a dark room, his candle shouldn't still have wax that is soft and warm. Additionally, the cup I picked up in the living room shouldn't have still been hot if it was made before bedtime.

Turns out Colin sleepwalks when stressed sometimes—and is quite busy. For whatever reason, he unwrapped the gifts while sleepwalking. He also made himself a fresh cup of tea. We decided to remove any candles or matches from his room, since he apparently used them while sleepwalking! From now on, only flashlights.

13. HOT COCOA HICCUP

Mrs. Claus is the thief. Even though she is lactose intolerant, she can't resist Santa's hot chocolate. The entire call she was trying to leave so she could go to the bathroom after guzzling down his last one. She also entered the room scratching her arm, which she states is also a side effect of her lactose intolerance. Santa agreed to start buying lactose-free cream just to make her special hot chocolate.

14. CONJURING CAPER

The assistant said he saw the burglar pick up a stack of ten- and twenty-dollar bills from the table in the center of the large library.

Had he not been guilty, he could not have known what the denominations of the bills were. It would have been impossible to have determined this from the doorway.

15. TOASTED TREE

In Mrs. Martindale's statement, she says that her husband "dragged the tree." Yet I only found footprints going out to the stump. My guess was that they lit last year's tree on fire for insurance purposes—it would take a lot for a fresh tree to burn that crispy. And the footprints were added as an extra detail.

After I questioned Mrs. Martindale further, she confirmed this theory. They wanted the insurance money to build a new deck.

WHAT'S NEXT

Did you enjoy these Christmas Mysteries?

Then you'll love the other Hailey Haddie
Minute Mystery books!

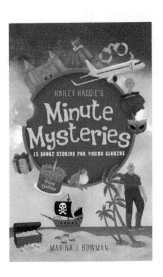 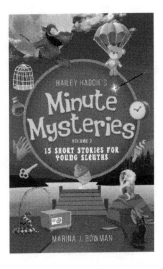

Continue the mystery-solving fun by visiting
scaredybat.com/minutemysteries

Want to sharpen your detective skills?

New Step-By-Step Guide to Solving Mysteries

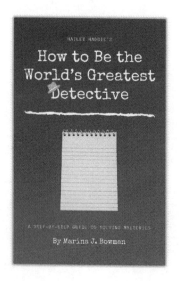

Learn how to become the world's greatest detective from the great Hailey Haddie!

Be first to know when it's released!
Visit <u>scaredybat.com/mm3-guide</u>

Discussion Questions

(1) What did you enjoy about these minute mystery stories?

(2) Which story was your favorite?

(3) What are some of the story themes?

(4) Were you able to solve the mysteries? If so, how?

(5) Detective Superpowers: Would you rather have x-ray vision or see details far away?

(6) What other books, shows, or movies do these stories remind you of?

(7) If you could talk to the author, what is one question you would ask her?

Dear Reader,

Hello there! Did you enjoy these short mystery stories? I know I did!

If you want to join the team as we solve more mysteries, then leave a review!

Otherwise, we won't know if you're up for the next case. And when we go to solve it, you may never hear about it!

You can leave a review wherever you found the book.

I'm excited to see you for the next mystery adventure!

Fingers crossed it's a super interesting one...

Yours Truly,
Detective Hailey Haddie

Also By Marina J. Bowman

SCAREDY BAT
A fear-busting vampire detective series
#1 Scaredy Bat and the Frozen Vampires
#2 Scaredy Bat and the Sunscreen Snatcher
#3 Scaredy Bat and the Missing Jellyfish
#4 Scaredy Bat and the Haunted Movie Set
#5 Scaredy Bat and the Mega Park Mystery
#6 Scaredy Bat and the Art Thief
#7 Scaredy Bat and the Dragon Necklace

HAILEY HADDIE MINUTE MYSTERIES
Solve-them-yourself supernatural mysteries

MISFIT MAGIC SCHOOL
Ember failed her magic exam...Now what?

THE LEGEND OF PINEAPPLE COVE
A mythical sea-faring adventure series

About the Author

MARINA J. BOWMAN is a writer and explorer who travels the world searching for wildly fantastical stories to share with her readers. She has always been fascinated with uncovering long lost secrets and chasing the mythical, magical, and supernatural.

Marina enjoys sailing, flying, and nearly all other forms of transportation. She stays away from the spotlight to maintain privacy and ensure the more unpleasant secrets she uncovers don't catch up with her.

As a matter of survival, Marina nearly always communicates with the public through her representative, Devin Cowick.

Made in the USA
Middletown, DE
11 December 2023